2/10

WWW.MYGOGIRLSERIES.COM

Get to know
the girls of

BY
MEREDITH BADGER

ILLUSTRATED BY
ASH OSWALD

FEIWEL AND FRIENDS
New York

A FEIWEL AND FRIENDS BOOK
An Imprint of Macmillan

Library of Congress Cataloging-in-Publication Data Available

ISBN-13: 978-0-312-34645-4
ISBN-10: 0-312-34645-X

First published in Australia by E2, an imprint of Hardie Grant Egmont.
Illustration and design by Ash Oswald.

First published in the United States by Feiwel and Friends,
an imprint of Macmillan.

Feiwel and Friends logo designed by Filomena Tuosto

First U.S. Edition: September 2008

10 9 8 7 6 5 4 3 2 1

www.feiwelandfriends.com

CHAPTER ONE

"OK, everyone," called Mr. Pcrelli above the noise. "Ten more problems to do in the last ten minutes!"

Sophie groaned.

This was the longest math lesson *ever*. Usually Sophie liked math, but today she couldn't concentrate.

"I wish the bell would ring," she whispered to her friend Alice.

"Me, too!" replied Alice. "I've got to finish packing for tomorrow."

Sophie felt a shiver of excitement. Tomorrow they were going to school camp. They were staying near a lake and would be going canoeing. Best of all, they were camping overnight!

"I wish it was just our class going," said Marie, who sat nearby. "Mrs. Tran's class

I can't wait to go camping!

is really stuck up. They're going to hate camping!"

"They'll probably freak out if they get a tiny bit of mud on them!" said Alice, laughing.

Sophie didn't know what to say. The thing is, she used to be in Mrs. Tran's class. She started school with those kids and she got to know them all really well. Her best friend Megan is in Mrs. Tran's class.

Sophie and Megan had always thought they would go right through school together. But two months ago the teachers decided to move some kids from each class. Sophie didn't know if she was excited or scared when Mrs. Tran told her she was one of them. Probably a little of both. Everyone in Mrs. Tran's class said that Mr. Perelli's class was rough and mean.

"The boys catch bugs," Megan said, wrinkling her nose. "Then they eat them."

"The girls hang from the monkey bars even when they're wearing dresses," said Katie. "They don't care if their undies are showing."

"And Mr. Perelli yells *all* the time," added Claire.

❀

Sophie's heart was beating fast when she walked into Mr. Perelli's class for the first time. Mr. Perelli was standing at the front of the classroom. He was frowning at something on the blackboard, but when he saw Sophie, he turned and smiled. It was a broad, friendly smile and it made his face look totally different.

"Hi, Sophie," he said. "Welcome to our class! There's a spare seat next to Alice. She'll look after you."

Sophie had seen Alice on the playground. She was tall and strong and spent most lunchtimes playing games. She always had scabs on her knees and grass stains on her clothes.

"She's so rough," Megan had said one day, as Alice went rushing past.

Sophie had nodded. Alice did look a little rough. But Sophie thought that she always looked like she was having fun.

Sophie might never have started talking to Alice if she hadn't made a spelling mistake in the very first class. She looked for her eraser but realized she had left it at home. Sophie didn't know what to do. If she had been in Mrs. Tran's class she would have asked Megan or Katie if she could borrow one. But she didn't know anyone in Mr. Perelli's class.

She suddenly felt very alone.

Then she felt a tap on her arm. It was Alice and she was holding out an eraser.

"Here," she said kindly. "Use mine. And

just get anything else you need out of my pencil case."

Sophie really looked at Alice for the first time. Alice had friendly brown eyes and a dimple in one cheek. Sophie took the craser. It was shaped like a strawberry and even smelled like one.

"Thanks!" Sophie said, and smiled at Alice.

✿

Ever since then, Sophie and Alice had been best friends. At least, they were best friends during class. But every lunchtime, Sophie went and found Megan.

"Don't you get bored hanging around with Megan all the time?" Alice asked one day.

Sophie shrugged. "A little," she said. "Sometimes."

Her Mrs. Tran friends liked to read magazines and chat. This was OK, but sometimes Sophie felt like running around with her new Mr. Perelli friends.

They always came back from lunch laughing about some new game they had invented. It would be nice to join in every now and then.

So one day, Sophie decided to play with Alice during lunch. She had a great time, and even made up a game that Alice said was the best thing she had ever played. But afterward Megan had been really upset.

"Do you like Alice more than me?" she asked.

Her voice sounded strange, like she was about to cry.

"Of course not," said Sophie.

She wanted to explain that she liked both of them, but she wasn't sure if this was what Megan wanted to hear.

Megan looked relieved. "I'm so glad you still like me the best!" she said, hugging Sophie.

After that, Sophie hadn't spent any more lunchtimes with Alice, even though Alice kept asking her to. It was weird. Sophie had always thought it would be nice having lots of people wanting to be your friend, but maybe it wasn't that great after all.

Whenever Sophie had a chance to make a wish, she wished for the same thing—that her friends would start liking each other. It would just make everything so much easier.

CHAPTER TWO

Finally, the bell rang and math was over. Everyone started talking and packing up. Mr. Perelli had to shout to be heard.

"Be here by eight o'clock tomorrow morning. If you're late, you'll be left behind."

Sophie decided she was going to be there at 7:30 a.m.

"Do you want to walk home with me?" asked Alice.

"I'm meeting Megan at the front gate," explained Sophie. "Maybe we could all walk home together?"

"No, that's OK," said Alice, quickly. "I just remembered something I have to do. I'll see you tomorrow."

Sophie sighed.

Why wouldn't her friends even *try* to like each other?

Megan was waiting by the gate. She was wearing a new outfit today, but that was no big surprise—Megan often had new clothes. Her mom worked for a fashion magazine and brought home lots of cool stuff. Not just clothes, either—she also brought CDs, posters, and nail polish.

Sophie never felt jealous though, because Megan was very generous. She gave lots of CDs to Sophie, and even some clothes. But somehow the clothes never looked as good on her as they did on Megan.

Megan was the sort of person that people turned around to stare at. Maybe it was her long, dark hair or her curly eyelashes. Perhaps it was her smile. Probably it was all of these things together.

When Sophie wore Megan's clothes she felt like a little kid dressing up. But when Megan put them on she looked like she should be in her mom's magazine.

Today Megan was wearing a pair of jeans turned up at the cuffs, a pink jacket, and a checkered hat. Sophie knew the hat would look stupid on her, but on Megan it looked cute. Under the hat though, Megan's face wasn't happy.

"I don't want to go on this dumb camping trip," she sighed, as they started to walk home.

"Why not?" asked Sophie, her heart sinking.

She felt like she could never find the right thing to say when Megan was in a bad mood.

"It's going to be cold and awful," said Megan. "Mrs. Tran said there isn't any electricity!"

"I've heard there aren't even any showers," said Sophie, without thinking.

Megan looked at her in horror. "No showers? That's gross!"

Sophie was actually looking forward to not taking a shower. It wouldn't matter if they got smelly because everyone else would smell, too.

"It won't be so bad," she said, trying to cheer Megan up. "It'll be like we're on *Survivor!*"

"That's what I'm afraid of," said Megan, gloomily.

Then Sophie remembered something Mr. Perelli had said that might make Megan happy.

"There's going to be a dance," she said. That worked.

"Really?" said Megan, actually smiling. "That might be OK, I guess."

Sophie had a feeling she knew why Megan was suddenly interested. She was imagining dancing with Joel Haddon.

Joel had spiky blond hair and green

eyes and lots of girls had secret crushes on him. Sophie didn't, though. She thought he was a big, fat pest.

The only person who was a bigger pest than Joel was his friend, Patrick Lee.

❋

"See you tomorrow!" Sophie said, when they arrived at Megan's house.

"Bye," said Megan. "Don't forget to bring snacks. The food will be terrible. Raisins and stuff." Megan made a face— she hated raisins.

"OK," said Sophie. "And don't worry about camp. I bet we'll have fun."

Megan snorted. "I'm glad you think so," she said. "I'm not so sure."

And deep down, Sophie wasn't so sure, either.

✿

CHAPTER THREE

Because it was the first half of the month, Sophie was living with her dad. She lived with her mom in the second half. This meant she had two of everything—two toothbrushes, two beds, and two desks. Other things, like her clothes, she had to pack up each time she switched houses.

"Hi, Dad!" yelled Sophie from the front door.

"Hi, Monster," her dad called back.

Monster was his nickname for her.

"Are you going to work in here with me this afternoon?" he called.

He was an illustrator and worked from home. Sophie liked making drawings on the floor of his studio while he worked at his desk.

"I can't today," said Sophie. "I have to pack!"

It didn't take her long. Sophie was an expert packer now.

Toothbrush. Toothpaste. Hairbrush. Raincoat. Boots. Thick socks. Undies. Sweater. Puffy jacket. Hat. T-shirt with cat on front. PJs. Sleeping bag. Pillow.

There was even some room left over.

thick socks

toothbrush

hat

boots

chips?

Just enough space for a bag of chips!

Sophie snuck into the kitchen to see if there were any in the pantry. Her dad didn't let her eat much junk food, so she would have to be sneaky. He was standing at the counter, chopping up vegetables for dinner.

"Come to give me a hand?" he asked, not looking up.

"I'll help in a sec," said Sophie.

She quietly opened the pantry.

Excellent! There was a big bag of chips right there.

The bag started to rustle loudly as she picked it up. Sophie quickly coughed to cover up the noise.

Her dad looked up and Sophie shoved the chips behind her back.

"Are you getting a cold?" he asked, looking worried.

"No, it's just a tickle in my throat," said Sophie.

Then she skipped off down the hall,

trying not to laugh. For once, she'd out-smarted her dad!

"By the way," he called out after her, "I bought you some chips to take to camp. They're in the pantry."

Sophie stopped and groaned.

How did her dad always know what she was up to? It was too weird.

Once she'd finished packing, Sophie helped her dad cook. They were having pasta and it was Sophie's job to make sure the spaghetti didn't stick together.

While she stirred the pot, Sophie started thinking. What if Megan was right about the food at camp? What if it was terrible?

Her mom always told her to just eat

the things she *did* like. But what if they served stuff she hated? Sophie only liked veggies that were crunchy. If they just served soggy cauliflower and mushy carrots she might starve!

Sophie usually told her dad about her day while they ate dinner, but tonight she was too busy worrying about camp to talk much. She might get homesick or stung by a bee. She might fall in the lake when they went canoeing. Was she a good-enough swimmer to make it to the shore?

"You must be so excited about going on your first camping trip, Monster," her dad said.

Sophie poked at her pasta. "I guess so," she said.

By the time she went to bed, Sophie had even more worries. What if she needed to go to the bathroom in the middle of the night? It would be pretty dark out there in the woods. It wasn't that she was afraid of the dark, but it was nice having a light switch nearby.

She curled up under her blanket and tried to fall asleep, but her eyes wouldn't close. Her backpack was casting a strange shadow on the wall. It looked a little like a bear. A big bear with pointy teeth and sharp claws.

Her dad came in to say good night.

If she told him she didn't want to go to camp anymore, would he let her stay home? She could help him work by sharpening his pencils and stuff like that.

Her dad sat on the end of her bed and handed her a small parcel. On it he had drawn a picture of a monster wearing a backpack.

"The monster looks worried," she said.

"It's a little nervous, but it's also excited," explained her dad. "Why don't you unwrap it and see what's inside?"

Sophie tore the wrapping off. Inside was a silver flashlight—small enough to fit in her pocket. Sophie turned it on. It was very bright.

The bear shadow on the wall completely disappeared.

"When I went on my first camping trip I kept a flashlight under my pillow," said her dad. "It kept me from feeling scared."

Sophie was surprised. She didn't think her dad was afraid of anything.

"I won't be scared," said Sophie, hugging her dad. Now that she had the flashlight, she knew it was true.

❋

CHAPTER FOUR

The next morning when Sophie's dad dropped her off, there was already a crowd outside the school. Two big buses were parked in the street.

"See you tomorrow!" said Sophie, giving her dad a kiss.

"Have a wonderful time, Monster," he said. "I'll miss you."

There was a lump in Sophie's throat as

he disappeared around the corner. For a horrible moment she thought she might cry, right in front of everyone.

Then she heard her name being called. Megan and Alice were already on one of the buses and they were waving to her from different windows. They both looked so excited that Sophie couldn't help feeling excited, too.

But once Sophie climbed on board she discovered something terrible. Both her friends had saved her a seat next to them. This was a big problem. Sophie stood in the doorway, not knowing what to do.

Then she felt a hand on her shoulder. It was Mrs. Tran.

"Hello, Sophie," she said, smiling. "Your mom just called to remind me that you get bus sick. You'd better sit up front with me."

Sophie turned red. Her mom could be really embarrassing sometimes. She was about to tell Mrs. Tran that she would be

OK sitting in the back when she thought of something. If she sat next to Mrs. Tran, then she wouldn't have to choose between her friends.

"OK," she said, feeling a little silly. "That's a good idea."

Sophie turned to Alice and Megan.

"Maybe you can sit next to each other?" she suggested.

"I should probably sit with Katie," said Megan.

"I'll sit next to Marie," said Alice.

The two girls changed seats. Sophie sighed. It was going to be a difficult day.

They hadn't gone very far when Sophie felt someone kicking her seat. She turned around and groaned when she saw who was there—Patrick Lee.

He grinned at her and stuck his finger up his nose. Sophie quickly turned away. How had she ended up sitting in front of the grossest, most annoying boy in the whole school?

It seemed like every week Patrick came up with a new way to annoy Sophie. Sometimes he threw paper planes at her head. Sometimes he made fart noises and pretended they came from her. Sometimes he made faces when it was her turn to read aloud. The faces he made were so strange that everyone who saw them couldn't help laughing.

Everyone except for Sophie. She didn't think they were funny at all.

The next time Patrick kicked the seat Sophie turned around and glared at him.

"If you don't stop doing that," she whispered angrily, "I'm going to tell Mrs. Tran."

Patrick's grin grew even wider.

He's so annoying!

"You wouldn't tell on me, would you?" he said.

"Don't be so sure," muttered Sophie.

Sophie knew that threats wouldn't normally stop Patrick, but luckily just then someone in the back started singing a bus song. Patrick stopped kicking and started singing instead.

It was sung to the tune of "Mary had a Little Lamb."

I know an annoying song
Annoying song
Annoying song
I know an annoying song
And this is how it goes.

When the kids reached the end they started again. It was the perfect song because it was very, very annoying!

Sophie could hear her friends singing in the back of the bus. She wished more than ever that she was sitting with them, having fun.

Mrs. Tran let them sing the song ten times in a row.

Then she said, "I know an annoying sentence. It goes like this: The next person who sings that song will be walking the rest of the way!"

Everyone stopped singing, but there was still some giggling from the back.

It didn't take long before Patrick

started kicking Sophie's seat again. She sighed.

It already felt like they had been driving for hours. How much longer was this going to take?

CHAPTER FIVE

Finally, the bus pulled off the dirt road and the campsite came into view. It was surrounded by tall, shady trees.

Nearby was a big lake with sparkling, clear water. On the shore was a row of brightly colored canoes.

Sophie was excited all over again. The horrible bus trip had been worth it. This was going to be a great camp.

Megan came up beside her.

"What a dump," she said, gloomily. "It's even worse than *Survivor*."

Sophie felt cross. Why did Megan always have to hate everything?

Mr. Perelli clapped his hands and called everyone over. Sophie stood between Alice and Megan.

"OK, everyone," he said. "I'm going to call out the tents now."

"Don't we get to pick?" Alice asked, sounding surprised.

"Not this time," said Mr. Perelli. "We've mixed up the classes so you get to know each other better."

Mr. Perelli started reading out names,

giving each group a tent.

"Tent number twelve," said Mr. Perelli, finally. "Sophie, Megan, and Alice."

The three girls stared at each other in shock. They stood there as if they had turned into statues. Sophie was the first to speak.

"Come on, guys," she said. "We'd better put up our tent."

This is terrible.

She picked up the tent bag and they set off in search of a spot to pitch the tent.

Sophie had always thought the worst tentmates would be people with smelly feet. Or people that snored. Or someone just plain gross like Patrick.

She would never have guessed that the worst people to share a tent with would be your two best friends.

CHAPTER SIX

The trouble started right away.

Alice had put up tents before and she started telling Sophie and Megan what to do. Sometimes Alice could be a little bossy. And she got annoyed when other people weren't as quick at doing things as she was.

"Sophie," said Alice, "hold up that pole."

Sophie picked up a pole.

"Not that one, birdbrain!" said Alice. "The short one."

Sophie didn't like being called a bird-brain, but she didn't say anything. She just wanted to get the tent up as quickly as possible.

"Now, Megan," said Alice, "you have to stretch out the rope really tight."

Megan glared at Alice. "I don't *have* to do anything," she said.

Alice glared back at Megan. "Yes, you do," she said. "Otherwise the tent will fall over."

Megan let go of the rope she was holding. "Good," she said. "I hope it does fall over—on your head!"

Alice's ears started to turn red and her mouth scrunched into a tight little line. Sophie knew what this meant. She had to do something—fast—before Alice exploded.

"Megan," she said, thinking quickly. "Could you ask Mr. Perelli for some extra tent pegs? We don't have enough."

For a moment Megan looked like she might refuse to go.

"OK," she sighed, after a moment. "But I'm doing it for *you*, Soph."

Once Megan had left, putting up the tent seemed much easier.

"Megan is such a pain," said Alice, as she hammered in tent pegs.

"She can be a bit of a brat sometimes," Sophie admitted.

Alice looked at Sophie in surprise. Normally Sophie stood up for Megan no matter what. But today she was feeling angry. It felt good to complain about Megan, just for once.

"I was getting so mad I wanted to tie her to a tree with the ropes!" giggled Alice.

Sophie giggled, too. "I don't think Megan would like that," she said. "The ropes wouldn't match her outfit."

The moment Sophie had said this, she felt bad. Megan was her oldest friend, after all.

When Sophie had failed a spelling test it was Megan who danced around all recess pretending to be a clown just to cheer her up. The day Sophie forgot her lunch, Megan gave her half of her own. And whenever Sophie stayed over, Megan always let her have the top bunk.

"I know Megan can be annoying,"

Sophie said, "but she can also be really funny and kind."

Alice didn't say anything, but Sophie could see that she didn't believe her.

After the tents had all been pitched, Mrs. Tran called everyone together again.

"We're going canoeing this afternoon," she said.

Alice grabbed Sophie's arm in excitement.

"There are some rules, though," said Mrs. Tran. "First, everyone must wear a life jacket."

At her feet was a pile of red life jackets.

"The second rule is no splashing or tipping other people's canoes. Anyone caught breaking this rule will have to get out of the lake. Is that clear?"

Everyone nodded.

"Finally, there are only two to a canoe."

Sophie looked around at Megan and Alice. Both of them were staring right at her.

"Come on, Soph," said Megan. "Who will you pick?"

CHAPTER
SEVEN

Luckily, Sophie remembered what her dad did when he couldn't make a decision. She felt in her pocket and found a quarter.

"I'll flip this coin," she explained to the others. "If it's heads, I'll go with Megan. Tails, Alice."

Megan and Alice nodded. This seemed fair. Sophie tossed the coin into the air and caught it. Heads!

"Yes!" said Megan, jumping up and down.

Alice shrugged. "Whatever," she said, walking away. "I'll just find someone else to go with."

Mrs. Tran gave out the life jackets and showed them how to put them on.

Megan scrunched up her face. "I don't want to wear that thing," she said, holding the life jacket away from her. "It looks horrible."

Sophie sighed. There were lots of kids already out on the lake in canoes, laughing and paddling around.

"It's not supposed to look good," Sophie said. "It's for safety. If you don't put it on, I'll go canoeing with Alice instead."

So Megan put on the life jacket.

Sophie looked at her and laughed.

"It actually kind of suits you," she said.

"Really?" said Megan.

Sophie nodded. It was typical. Even a life jacket looked cool on Megan!

Everyone else was on the lake by the time Megan and Sophie finally got their canoe into the water.

Mr. Perelli canoed over to give them some tips.

"Paddle in time with each other," he called out to them. "One stroke on each side will make you go in a straight line."

Sophie got the hang of it right away but

Megan found it hard. She kept paddling on the same side and the canoe started going around in circles.

Sophie started to feel very frustrated.

But Megan wasn't listening. It was like pitching the tent all over again.

Alice and Marie paddled over, looking

like they'd been canoeing all their lives.

"Isn't this fun?" said Alice. Her face was glowing.

"No," said Megan, grumpily. "It's boring and stupid."

Alice and Marie looked at Megan in surprise. Sophie was embarrassed—she wished Megan wouldn't say stuff like that.

Suddenly, from nowhere, raindrops pattered onto the girls' heads.

Sophie looked up at the sky, but it was perfectly clear. What was going on? Then Sophie heard someone laughing. It was a laugh she knew only too well.

Patrick paddled up beside them. He was sharing a canoe with Joel Haddon.

When Megan saw him she smiled for the first time since they had arrived at camp.

"Hi, Joel!" she said, waving.

She opened her mouth to say more, but before she could speak the rain fell again. Except it wasn't rain at all—it was Patrick.

He scooped his paddle through the water and another shower came pouring down on the girls' heads.

"Hey, no splashing!" Sophie shouted.

Patrick grinned. "What are you going to do?" he said. "Tell?"

"What do you think?" Sophie whispered to Megan. "Should I tell Mr. Perelli?"

Megan shrugged. "Let's just splash him

back," she said.

Before Sophie could say anything, Megan started splashing the boys. Unfortunately, most of the water landed on Alice and Marie.

"Hey!" yelled Alice, and started splashing back at Megan.

"Stop it!" cried Sophie, and tried to grab Megan's paddle. Somehow, in the struggle, she ended up splashing the boys even more.

None of them noticed that Mr. Perelli had appeared beside them in his canoe.

"Girls! What did we say about splashing?" he said, sounding angry.

Sophie looked at him in horror. "It was an accident, Mr. Perelli," she said.

"It didn't look like an accident to me," he said. "You heard the rules. You four will have to get out."

Sophie felt tears welling in her eyes as they paddled to the shore. She couldn't believe this was happening.

"Well, that's a relief," said Megan as

they pulled the canoe out of the water. "I didn't want to go canoeing anyway."

Alice was beside her.

She looked mad. *Really* mad.

"Maybe *you* didn't want to go canoeing," she said, "but *we* all did. We were really looking forward to it."

"All you ever think about is what *you* want, Megan," Alice went on. "You've wrecked the whole trip for the rest of us."

Megan looked shocked. She opened her mouth to speak but nothing came out.

Alice put her hands on her hips. She had more to say.

"I can't understand why Sophie is friends with you. All you care about is clothes."

I am
sick of this:

Megan folded her arms. "I do NOT just care about clothes," she said. "And I can't understand why Sophie is friends with you. You're so bossy!"

Sophie looked at her two friends yelling at each other. It was then that she realized she'd had enough. She was sick and tired of always being in the middle.

"You can stop fighting about who I should be friends with, because I've decided for myself," she said.

Alice and Megan both got quiet. For once they were actually listening to her.

Sophie took a deep breath. "I don't want to be friends with *either* of you anymore."

Then she turned and ran away.

✻

CHAPTER EIGHT

There was a big tree in her dad's back-
yard, and whenever Sophie felt angry she
climbed it. She was good at climbing and
being up high always made her feel better.

So after the fight, Sophie went and
found the tallest tree at the campsite and
climbed until she was high above the tents.
From up there she could see the kids on
the lake, canoeing around.

She was still upset but she felt much better being in the tree. How long could she stay up here? Maybe she could even sleep on one of the branches, holding onto the trunk. Sophie was just wondering if she should go and get her sleeping bag when she heard a voice from down below her.

It was Alice.

"Please come down, Sophie," she said. "I'm sorry I made you mad."

Alice sounded really upset, but Sophie didn't answer her. She stared at the lake instead. When she looked down, Alice had gone. But a few minutes later she heard another voice.

This time it was Megan.

"This is dumb, Soph," she said. "Come down so we can at least talk about it."

"Go away," said Sophie. "I'm staying here."

Then she heard new footsteps. Someone else was coming to annoy her. Why couldn't they all just leave her alone?

"Sophie Stewart! What are you doing?"

Sophie looked down. Oops! It was Mrs. Tran, and she looked mad.

"You are on dinner duty tonight," said Mrs. Tran. "I expect you down here in exactly one minute."

Mrs. Tran could be very scary sometimes. Sophie climbed down right away.

"If you do anything like this again, I'll have to send you home," said Mrs. Tran. "Now, go and help the others with dinner."

"Yes, Mrs. Tran," said Sophie.

❁

Alice and Megan had already started serving food when Sophie arrived.

Sophie took her place between them. Alice was putting hot dogs on the plates as the kids walked by in a line. Megan added a dollop of mashed potatoes. Sophie's job was to give each person a scoop of peas.

The three girls worked side by side but didn't talk to each other.

Sophie concentrated on giving out scoops of peas. She was thinking about how she would probably be angry with Alice and Megan forever when she heard a funny noise.

It sounded disgusting—wet and

squelchy. At first, Sophie couldn't figure out where it was coming from. Then she realized that it happened every time Megan put mashed potatoes on a plate. Sophie looked at Megan.

Megan smiled and made the noise again by sucking on the inside of her cheek. It was a really gross sound.

Sophie wanted to laugh, but if she laughed she knew she wouldn't be angry anymore. She bit the corners of her mouth to stop them from curling up. Then she caught a glimpse of Alice, who had a big grin on her face.

Megan made the sound again as a big scoop of potatoes hit the plate. Alice giggled, although she looked like she was trying hard not to.

Patrick was next in line.

Sophie didn't feel like serving Patrick any dinner.

Hmmmm...
Patrick
is hungry?

"I'm starving!" said Patrick, holding out his plate. "Give me lots of food."

Alice looked at Sophie and gave her a wink. She picked up the smallest hot dog in the tray and put it on Patrick's plate.

Sophie smiled. She knew what Alice had in mind. Sophie carefully dropped five peas next to the tiny hot dog. Then Megan gave him a teaspoonful of mashed potatoes.

Patrick looked down at his plate. "Hey!" he said. "How come I got such a small serving?"

"Because you're a big pest," said Megan.

"But I'm starving!" said Patrick, crossly.

"Oh," said Megan, "then have some more!"

She scooped up an enormous dollop of mashed potatoes.

Splat!

The potatoes covered all the other food on Patrick's plate. They splashed over

Patrick's clothes. Some of them even stuck to his chin so he looked like he had a potato beard! There were lots of potatoes on Megan, too, but she didn't seem to care.

"Is that enough?" asked Megan, "or would you like some more?"

Sophie burst out laughing. She couldn't help it. Patrick looked so funny with potatoes dripping off his chin. All the laughter she'd been squashing down came bubbling out. Alice laughed, too.

Soon all three girls were laughing so hard they could hardly breathe.

Patrick looked down at his huge plate of potatoes. For a moment Sophie thought that he was going to get angry. But instead he did something Sophie wasn't expecting—he started laughing, too.

He kept laughing as he walked away with potatoes still stuck on his chin.

Sophie couldn't believe it. For once it seemed that Patrick Lee didn't have something smart to say.

CHAPTER nine

Once the girls had started laughing, it seemed stupid not to talk to each other.

"That was the funniest thing I've seen in ages," said Sophie.

"Me, too," said Alice, holding her stomach. "I've got a stitch."

She looked at Sophie. "Are you still mad?" Alice asked.

Sophie shook her head. "Nope," she said.

"I'm sorry about yelling," Alice said to Megan. Then she kicked at the ground. "I guess I get jealous sometimes because you're Sophie's oldest friend."

Megan shrugged. "Well, I get jealous because you're her newest friend!"

Sophie stared at her friends in surprise. It had never crossed her mind that this might be the cause of all the problems.

Mrs. Tran came over. "Make sure you have some dinner, too," she said. "But be quick! The dance starts soon. Don't forget the theme is Outer Space."

The dance!

Sophie had forgotten all about it.

Once Mrs. Tran had gone, the three

girls examined the leftover food. It didn't look very good. The hot dogs were cold. The peas had gone all wrinkly and the mashed potatoes were really runny.

Then Sophie had an idea. "I've got chips," she said. "Let's have those instead."

Megan nodded. "Cool. I've got cookies and chocolate. What about you, Alice?"

Alice shook her head. "I haven't got anything."

"Nothing at all?" asked Megan.

Alice looked embarrassed. "Just raisins. My mom doesn't buy junk food."

"That's OK," said Megan. "I *love* raisins!"

Alice looked surprised. "Really?" she asked.

Megan nodded. "Really. They'll be perfect for our feast."

Sophie kept quiet. She knew Megan was lying about liking raisins but she was glad. It was a good lie.

In the tent the girls spread out their food and started to eat. They were all really hungry. Megan even ate a couple of raisins, but Sophie noticed that she quickly had a chip afterwards.

"Now," said Megan, once they had finished. "What should we wear to the dance?"

Sophie thought about the stuff she had packed. There was nothing that was right.

"Can't we just go like we are?" asked Alice.

Megan looked shocked. "Of course not! You have to dress up," she said.

"But I didn't bring anything," said Sophie.

"Me, either," said Alice.

Megan reached over and opened up her backpack. Clothes of all shapes and colors came spilling out.

"Lucky I did then!" she laughed.

Megan picked out a shimmery silver top and matching silver skirt for Alice to wear.

Alice looked at them doubtfully. "I don't think these will even fit me," she said.

"Yes, they will," said Megan.

Alice tried them on and they fit perfectly.

"How do I look?" Alice asked shyly.

"Great!" Sophie and Megan said at the same time. It was true. The top looked amazing on Alice. It made her eyes sparkle.

Megan found Sophie a black top covered in tiny gold stars and a pair of black pants with gold thread. Sophie had never worn anything like this before.

Once they were both dressed, Megan said, "Now for some makeup."

She pulled a big pink bag out of her backpack. Inside were hundreds of make-up samples from her mom's work.

"Try this," said Megan, holding out a little silver jar to Sophie and Alice.

It was pink, sparkly lip gloss that smelled like peaches. Alice and Sophie stuck their fingers in and put some on their lips.

"This one is for your eyelids," said Megan, handing over another little com-pact. It was filled with silver eye shad-ow. She got the girls to shut their eyes while she put it on for them.

"You start from the inside of the lid and work across to the outside," she explained.

When she had finished, Sophie and Alice looked at each other.

"You look so much older!" Sophie said to Alice.

"So do you!" said Alice. "You look totally different."

Sophie wished she could see herself. She had never worn much makeup before. In the distance, they could hear music playing.

"It's started!" said Megan, jumping up. "Let's go."

"But you're not ready," said Sophie.

Megan's top was still covered in dried-up potatoes.

"Oh yeah, I forgot," said Megan.

She picked up the lip gloss and quickly dabbed some on her lips. Then she gave her clothes a quick brush with her hands. Some of the potato came off but lots of it stayed stuck on.

"OK, I'm ready," she said, and climbed out of the tent.

Alice and Sophie followed behind.

"You know," Alice said to Sophie, "normally I hate all that makeup and dressing up stuff. But that was fun."

"Yeah," nodded Sophie. "It was, wasn't it?"

CHAPTER TEN

Sophie gasped when she saw the clearing where the dance was being held. Someone had been very busy decorating. Silver stars and moons hung from the branches, sparkling and twinkling when the breeze blew through them. The tree trunks were wrapped up with streamers and the grass had been sprinkled with glitter.

It looked almost magical.

Mr. Perelli had brought the school's battery-powered stereo and it was playing loudly beneath one of the trees.

There were already lots of kids there, but no one was dancing—everyone was standing around the edge looking embarrassed. Megan grabbed Sophie and Alice.

"Come on!" she said, "Let's be first."

"I'm no good at dancing," Alice said nervously, as Megan dragged her onto the dance floor. "Maybe I should just watch."

But Megan shook her head. "No way! Of course you can dance. Anyone can. Just move around like this."

Megan started dancing, and Sophie

joined in, too. She felt a little silly at first, but the more she did it, the better she felt.

"Come on, Alice!" Sophie said. "It's fun. I promise."

So Alice started dancing. She looked kind of funny. Her arms were moving around too quickly. She looked like she had bugs in her shirt that were tickling her.

Sophie almost started laughing, but Megan stamped on her foot.

"Ouch!" said Sophie, hopping around.

Megan frowned at her. "Don't laugh," she whispered, "or Alice will give up."

Sophie nodded. Megan was right.

It wasn't long before Alice got the hang of it and was dancing just as well as Megan and Sophie.

"Hey!" she said, after a while. "This *is* fun."

Once the other kids saw Sophie, Megan, and Alice dancing, they started going onto the dance floor, too.

Soon everyone was dancing—even Mrs. Tran and Mr. Perelli!

Alice knew all the words to every song. Sophie and Megan were surprised—they didn't know Alice liked pop music.

"Do you know this band?" Megan asked Alice.

Alice nodded. "X-Press—my sister has the CD."

"The boys in the band are *so* cute," said Megan, "don't you think?"

Alice turned red. "I have a poster of them on my bedroom wall," she admitted.

Wow!
My friends are
getting along!

"Cool!" said Megan. "I'd love to see it."

Sophie couldn't help smiling. Megan and Alice had things in common after all!

"Hey, watch me!" said Sophie, and she did a spin. When she stopped spinning she found she was staring right into Patrick Lee's face. He must have been standing right behind her.

"Hi," he said.

"Go away," said Sophie, and she started

to turn her back on him.

"Hang on," said Patrick. "I've got something to say."

For once he actually sounded serious.

"What?" asked Sophie.

She would give him ten seconds, but that was all.

"I'm sorry about wrecking the canoeing. I didn't mean to get you into trouble," said Patrick.

Sophie looked at him suspiciously. She waited for him to start laughing or to tell her she'd been tricked.

But he didn't.

"Really?" she asked.

Patrick nodded. "Yep," he said. "I

started thinking about what happened while I ate *all* those potatoes. So I told Mr. Perelli the whole story and he said that he'd take you and the others canoeing tomorrow."

Sophie didn't know what to say. Had Patrick actually done something nice for a change? He had never been anything more than a big pain. Now he was standing there with an expression Sophie had never seen on his face before.

He looked sorry.

"Thanks, Patrick," Sophie said, smiling. "That's really cool."

When Sophie turned back to her friends they wanted to hear the gossip. They couldn't believe it when Sophie told them what he'd done.

"You know," said Megan, "Patrick looks a little like one of the boys from X-Press. And he's a pretty good dancer, too."

Sophie sneaked a look at Patrick, who had gone back to his friends. Well, Megan was half right—Patrick *was* a good dancer. But he definitely didn't look like a pop star to Sophie!

When they stopped to take a break, Mr. Perelli came over.

"So, who is going canoeing tomorrow?" he asked.

Sophie looked nervously at her friends.

"Soph, you should go with Alice this time," said Megan.

Sophie gave her friend a hug. "Thanks, Megan," she said. "You didn't really like canoeing anyway, did you?"

"Actually," said Megan, "by the end I was sort of enjoying it. Maybe I'll go with

Katie tomorrow—I might get the hang of it with a little more practice."

A new song started playing on the stereo.

"Come on!" said Alice. "We *have* to dance to this one!"

And she dragged Megan and Sophie back onto the dance floor.

They kept dancing until the batteries ran out on the stereo. By the time they crawled into their tent, their arms and legs ached, and their throats were sore from nonstop singing. It was very dark in the tent.

Sophie wriggled into her sleeping bag easily but she could hear the other two scuffling around, bumping into each other in the darkness.

"I think my pajamas have shrunk," said Megan. Her voice was muffled.

"There is something seriously wrong with my sleeping bag," said Alice, sounding confused.

Sophie suddenly remembered the present her dad had given her. She felt under her pillow for her flashlight and turned it on. She couldn't help laughing at what she saw.

Megan had put her pajama pants over her head and Alice was trying to climb into her backpack!

Sophie put the flashlight near the entrance to the tent.

"I'll leave it here in case anyone needs

it during the night," she laughed.

Although Sophie was exhausted, she couldn't fall asleep right away. She kept thinking about all the things that had happened. Megan must have been thinking about the same stuff.

Her voice drifted up through the darkness. "I can't believe we've only been here one day," she said. "It feels so much longer."

"I know," said Alice. "What was your favorite part?"

"Definitely the dance," said Megan. "But dinner in the tent was fun, too. What about you, Sophie?"

Sophie thought about it for a moment.

She remembered the bus ride and the canoeing and the fight. She thought about Patrick's mashed potato beard and getting ready for the dance and dancing until she was ready to drop.

And she thought about how the thing she had always hoped for finally seemed to be happening. Her friends were getting along.

"I loved it all," she said. "Every single minute."

And she meant it.

THE END